To small friends the world over

Library of Congress Cataloging-in-Publication Data:
Fujikawa, Gyo. Are you my friend today? SUMMARY: Special friends have fun together
playing, talking, and sharing. [1. Friendship—Fiction] I. Title. PZ7.G9513Ar 1988 [E]
88-3224 ISBN: 0-394-89031-0 (trade); 0-394-99031-5 (lib. bdg.)

Manufactured in the United States of America   1 2 3 4 5 6 7 8 9 0

Are You My Friend Today?

GYO FUJIKAWA

RANDOM HOUSE 🏠 NEW YORK

Hi! Are You My Friend Today?

Let's play, you and me, let's talk.
Let's go find the other kids.
Maybe we can all play together....

We Are Friends!

Here we are, all good friends!
We spend our days together
having lots of fun.

We are going to catch some fish.

We like
to share....

Time to smell
the flowers.

Watch out,
Mr. Squirrel,
here we come!

Can we talk?

Up we go!

Down we go!

Up!
Down!
Up and
down!

Glub, glub,
join me for a swim!

Running barefoot   feels s-o-o-o good!

We are taking
the children for a walk.

Come on,
let's splash!

Hi, bird!
Wouldn't you
like to swing
with me?

Tra-la-la
and la!

Look out below!

Big treats and
little treats make
us feel so good inside.
Tell us, what makes you
feel wonderful?

I love
a picnic in
the backyard.

Our Monster

Away we go,
  chasing our
  gigantic monster.
We're not afraid of him.
  We love him.
Because, you see,
  he's just pretend.
Our monster is a dinosaur
  and very ancient.
He's at least
  a zillion years old!

It's a Bad Day

When you fall out
    of bed the first thing
    in the morning,
        it's a bad day!

Or if you step on your dog's tail
(by mistake, of course)...

When you spill ice cream
    on your brand-new dress...

When you bat a ball
and conk your best friend
on the head...
it's a bad day.

If you stub your toe
on a dumb old rock...

When you slip
on a banana peel
and look silly!...

When you get mixed up
in a big argument...
it's a very bad day!

Oh, well,
there's always
tomorrow...
I know it'll be
a very good day!

School Time

Mustn't be late for school!
It's time for learning
and time for playing—
lots of playing!

Make-Believe Zoo

Come and look for us
    in our make-believe zoo.
We are creatures of the wild,
    and we are waiting for you!

So come and visit us.
    Who knows—
    maybe you, too,
Can be a bird or a beast
    in our make-believe zoo.

Here Comes the Mailman!

Guess what?
 We are making our
 own cards this year!

After
 Mama writes the addresses
 on the envelopes, we'll lick
 the stamps and stick them on.

Next
 we run to the mailbox
 and send them to friends
 far and near.

Then
before you know it, here comes
the mailman and he has something
for US!

Look! Look!
He's brought lots and lots
of cards from all our friends,
wishing us
"Happy Holidays!"

Anything for us?

Deep Feelings

Everybody has all kinds of feelings,
    not just good feelings
        but bad feelings too.
Lonely feelings
    and sad feelings,
Angry feelings
    and friendly feelings.
Disappointed feelings
    and stuck-up feelings.
And there are unhappy feelings
    as well as the best—
        <u>happy</u> feelings!

You're not our
friend today!

I'm sorry...

Sprinkle, sprinkle,
come my way.
I would love to
soak all day!

Drizzle, drizzle, go away,
must you spoil our game today?

I don't like you!

Who cares?

My puppy
ran away!

See! We're
good friends
again!

Doing It Your Way

There comes a time when
you must do things
all by yourself
in your own way.

I can
walk!

I'm ready to go!
How do I look?

Isn't my hair
just
gorgeous?

Teeth, teeth,
here
I come!

Why does Johnny think I need a bath?

My brother likes to
sleep in the doghouse.
How come?

MR. DOG

But I like
my shoes on this way.

How did I do that?

I'm the best
sandwich maker in the
whole wide world!

Here,
kitty,
kitty,
kitty!

All Year Long with the Twins

January

February

May

June

September

October

March

April

July

August

November

December

A Mystery

Teddy bear is missing!
    All day long we search
    high and low for him.
Finally we see him, perched
    among the leaves
    way, way up in the treetop.
Now the big question is,
    how did he get up there?
It's a mystery!

After all, Teddy can't
    climb like a real live bear.

But there he is
    in the treetop.
Somebody or something
    got him there. Who?

Maybe the wind blew him up there.

Maybe one of us put him in the tree.

The next morning we run
     to the tree, and guess what!
There is Teddy under the tree,
     sitting on the ground!

Now there are two mysteries.
     How did Teddy get
          up in the tree
          and how did he
          get down?

Do you know?

For the answer, turn the book upside down.

By Myself

Sometimes,
    for no reason
    in particular,
I climb a tree....
    I just like to sit
    up there
    by myself
and think a whole lot
    about nothing
    much at all.

A Very Special Friendship

I have a friend,
    a secret friend.
Nobody knows my friend
    but me.
Nobody can see my friend
    but me.
How I love
    my very own,
    my special,
    my secret friend!

Pet Parade

Let's have a parade,
  everybody!
Let's show off our pets.
  Ever-loving,
  ever-faithful,
they deserve their own
  special parade.
  Don't you agree?

Let's show the world
  we love our pets as
  much as they love us.
So join the parade,
  everybody!
And shout to the skies,
  "Hooray
  for P-E-T-S!"

The Birthday Party

Yummy, yummy, yummy!
Today is my birthday!
All my friends have come
to help me eat
this great, big, beautiful
birthday cake!
Yummy, yummy, yummy!

Sleepover Time! Look at us! Shouting and laughing,
we jump up and down! What fun!

Then, oh so tuckered out, we plop down to
sleep and dream of happy tomorrows!

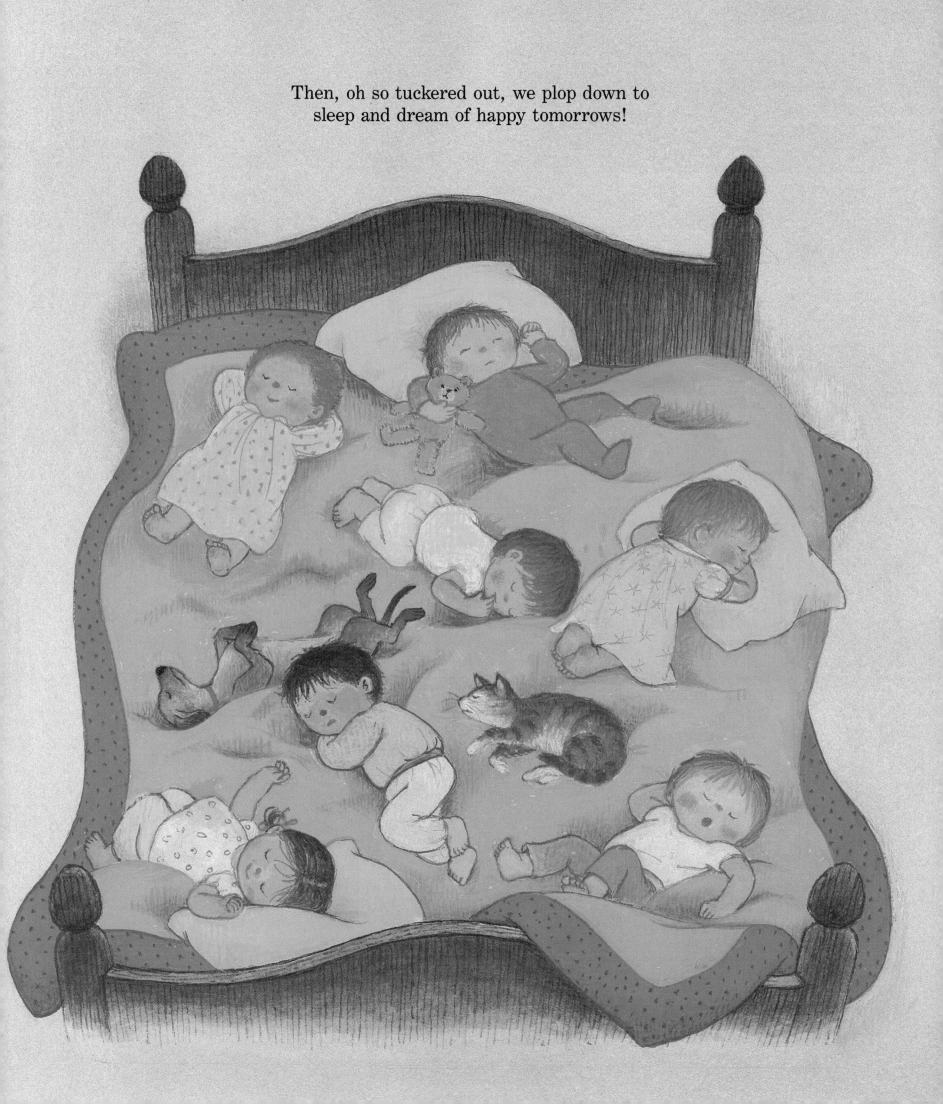

So Long for Now!

Let's play again tomorrow.
Remember, we're friends
forever and forever!